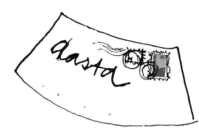

To my own Bjorn.

Copyright © Stina Langlo Ørdal 1999

Published by Bloomsbury, New York and London
Distributed to the trade by St. Martin's Press
Library of Congress Cataloging-in-Publication Data:
Ordal, Stina Langlo.
Princess Aasta / Stina Langlo Ordal. p.cm.
Summary: Princess Aasta and her new friend, a polar bear named Kvitejorn, play in the garden, travel to
the North Pole, and have supper with the king.
ISBN 1-58234-783-2
[1. Friendship--Fiction. 2. Princesses—Fiction. 3. Polar bear—Fiction. 4. Bears--Fiction] I. Title.
PZ7.06253 Pr 2002 [E]—dc21   2001056462
First U.S. Edition 2002

Printed in Hong Kong by South China Printing Co.

1 3 5 7 9 10 8 6 4 2

Bloomsbury USA Children's Books
175 Fifth Avenue
New York, New York 10010

Princess Aasta

by Stina Langlo Ørdal

BLOOMSBURY
CHILDREN'S
BOOKS

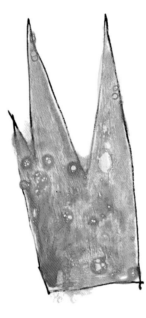

Once upon a time
there was a little princess
called **Aasta,**
who wanted a bear
to love.

She decided to send a letter to a newspaper – "Little princess seeking big, cuddly bear friend."

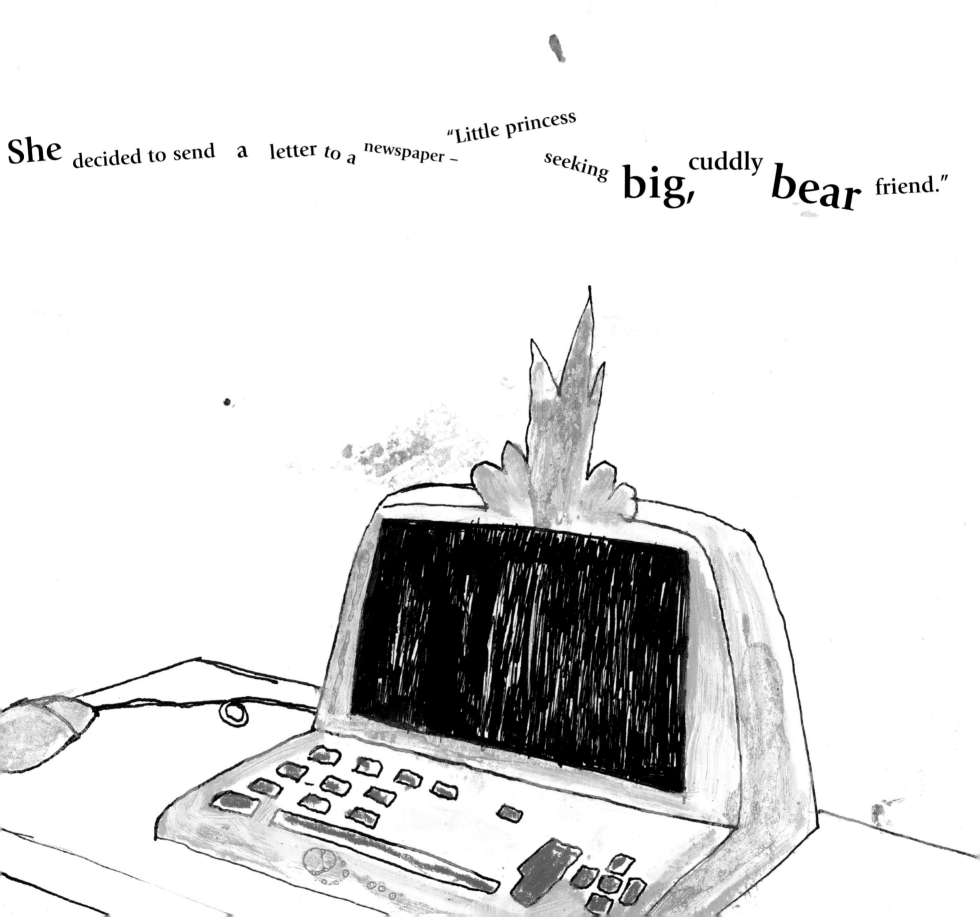

Shortly afterwards, she **received** letters from **bears** all over the **world.**

Black, brown and white bears, and even grizzly bears.

Princess Aasta was very excited and went through

all the letters

(there were many of them).

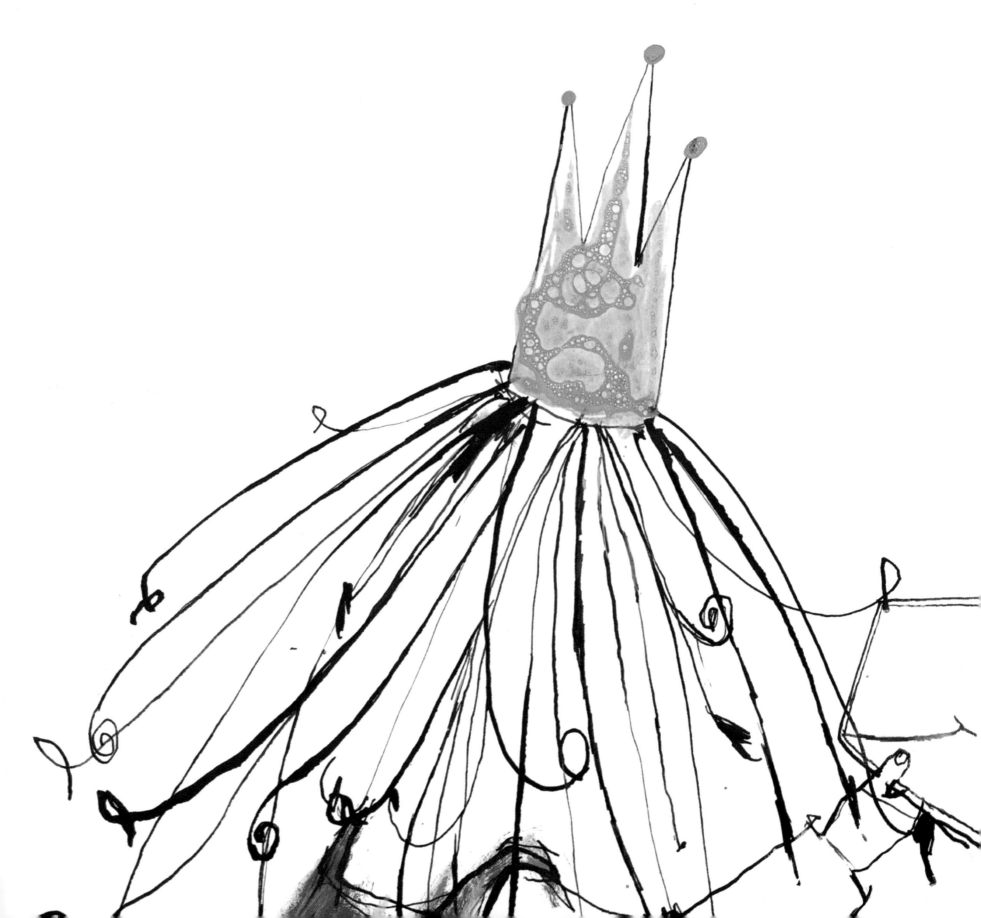

She chose one, Kvitebjørn, who had the friendliest eyes she had ever seen, and sent a letter back to him asking if they could meet some time.

They met in Princess Aasta's apple garden, and chased each other in between the trees.

Kvitebjørn picked apples for Princess Aasta from the top branches.

Princess Aasta and Kvitebjørn wanted to be together always.

The **King** was worried about having a **big,** dangerous Ursus maritimus running about in his garden.

But when he saw how much **fun** the two of them had together, he left them alone.

And when Kvitebjørn wanted to take Princess Aasta on a day trip to the North Pole, where he was from, the King couldn't say no.

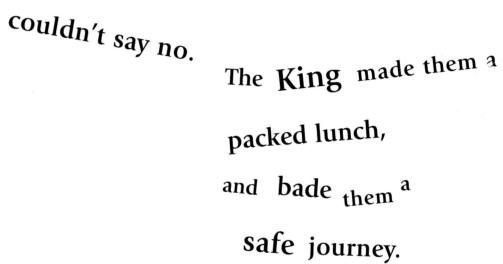

The King made them a packed lunch, and bade them a safe journey.

Princess Aasta climbed on to Kvitebjørn's back, and off they went, as far north as anyone can get. It was so beautiful up there, everything was covered in ice and snow. And Princess Aasta would never be cold, because Kvitebjørn's fur kept her warm.

Kvitebjørn introduced her to all his polar bear friends.

Afterwards, they went ice-skating and made an enormous snowman together.

And when northern lights appeared in the sky, it was time to go back to the King's castle.

The King was waiting for them at the door.

He was still a bit scared of Princess Aasta's huge polar bear friend, but when Kvitebjørn bent down and gave him a

huge, warm and cuddly hug,

he felt a bit better and asked if Kvitebjørn

would join them for supper.

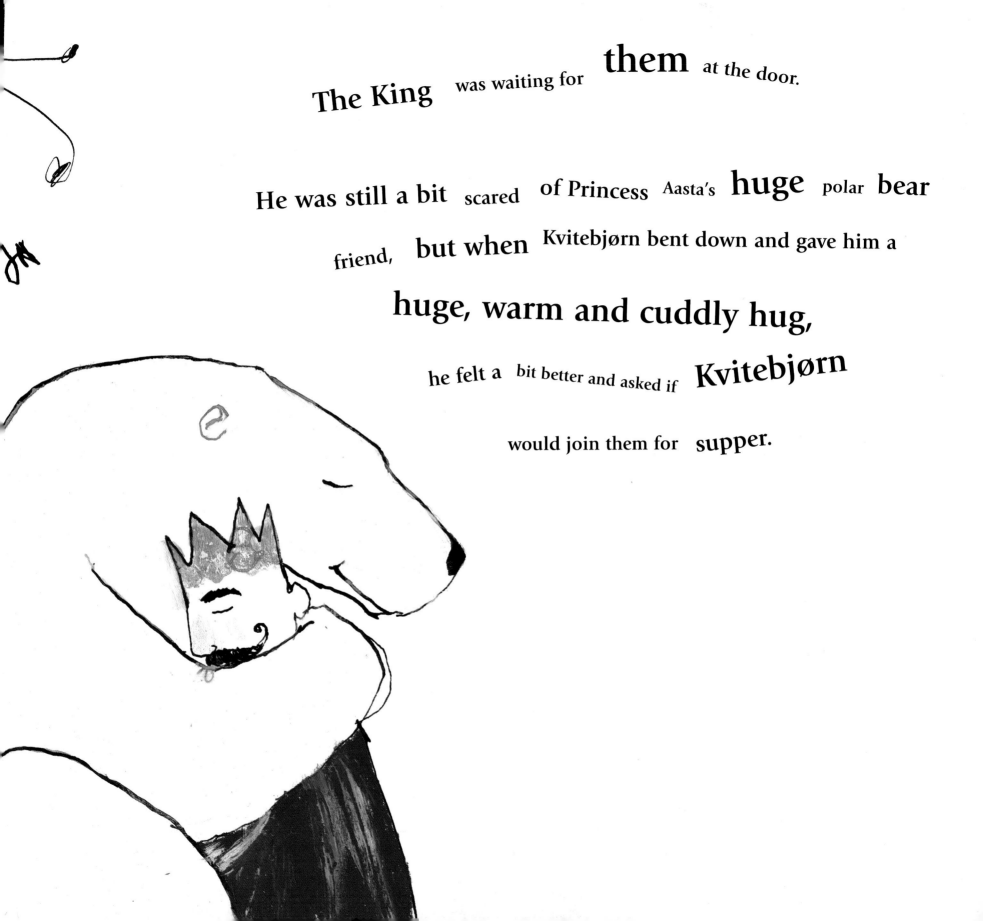